From Alone
A Home

a collection of shelter stories

1

A Dog Called
Meatball
And His Brother Chicken Nugget

Lisa Spaulding
Bonnie Wiegand

ISBN-13: 978-1724739315

ISBN-10: 172473931X

These stories, which are inspired by true events, are dedicated to all the amazing animals patiently awaiting forever homes in animal shelters worldwide.

Table of Contents

1

They Were Survivors

The rain had finally stopped and two little black noses slowly slid out from under a down-turned plastic crate. With a couple bops the crate flipped over and out popped a couple of young black and tan puppies. With their noses to the ground they sniffed their way around the alley until they found their favorite dumpster. Littered throughout the street were pizza crusts and breadstick crumbs waiting to be lapped up. The pups did just that.

"Get out of here, you mangy mutts!"
barked an angry human. They had found an
easy meal this time, but that wasn't always the
case.

Meet Rudy and Ruger! They are brothers and soon after they were born they found themselves living out on the streets. These two stray, homeless dogs were two of many. However, they were survivors. They adapted and learned how to live on their own. They found shelter when the weather turned stormy, and they found food when they were hungry. But, a lot of dangers lurk for stray dogs.

Cars are a huge threat to the safety of these boys. It doesn't matter how many cars come to a screeching halt to avoid them. They will never learn to look both ways before crossing the street.

"Rudy! Rudy! I bet you can't catch me!" shouted Ruger.

"I'm coming for you, Ruger!"
Without hesitation the young pups cruised out from the alley and across the busy road to their favorite park. They were completely unaware of the cars that swerved to miss their furry little bodies.

The risk for illness and injury are high as well for strays like these two. Without access to a veterinarian, even a minor wound can lead to disaster.

"Ruger! Ruger! Help! I'm stuck!" cried Rudy.

"I'm coming brother! I'll get you out!" hollered Ruger.

Ruger followed his brother's calls to find him whimpering at the edge of a pond. Rudy's leg was caught in fishing line and the hook was stuck in his paw! Ruger was able to pop the hook out and luckily it wasn't wedged in too deep. Rudy licked his wounds until he felt better. Fortunately, he healed quickly and it did not become infected.

Finding nutritious food and clean water, and finding enough of each is a constant battle for these dogs.

"Rudy, I'm hungry," moaned Ruger.

"Me too. The dumpster is empty. We'll look again in the morning," whispered Rudy.

They curled into two tiny balls and dozed off under the stars, their tummies rumbling.

They were still young and the dangers of the surrounding world were far from their minds. This was all they had ever known. They didn't know what it meant to be part of a family. But at least they had each other, for now anyway.

2
Something Big

One summer day, as Rudy and Ruger
were playing in their favorite field, a man with
a bag of tempting treats came out of nowhere.
They looked at each other and decided to
check it out. The man fed them treat after
treat and the boys followed him back to his
car.

"Come on, boys! Come with me! Let's get you off the street and out of harm's way!"

Rudy, being the more trusting of the pair, hopped into the back of the man's car. Ruger, on the other hand, was much more cautious. He ducked away from the man and darted in the opposite direction. The man figured saving one puppy was better than none and drove away.

Ruger sat with his head at a tilt as he watched his brother, his friend, and his only companion in the world speed off. Rudy sat in the back of the unfamiliar car watching his brother, his friend, and his only companion in the world become smaller and smaller in the distance. It didn't take long for Rudy or Ruger to figure out that something big had just happened.

Soon the man with the treats pulled his car into the parking lot of a large building. He opened the back door and Rudy hopped out as the man looped a leash around Rudy's skinny neck. At this point, Rudy became nervous, but with the leash connecting him to this man, he had no choice but to follow him inside the strange building.

"I found this puppy running along the highway and wanted to get him to a safe place. I hope he has a family out there looking for him. There was another pup with him, but I couldn't catch him," said the man with the treats to the woman behind the desk.

"Thank you so much for your concern and your time. He is safe here and we will have the Animal Control officers keep an eye out for his buddy. We hope someone calls looking for him, but if no one claims him in the next week, he will become available for adoption. Thanks again for your help today!"

Another staff member smiled and took control of the leash connected to Rudy. Rudy was scared and repeatedly looked over his shoulder, hoping he would see Ruger stroll in behind him. No such luck.

The girl led him through a door to a room full of numerous dogs all in their own kennels. Some were lying down, some were barking at the gate, some were chewing on a bone, but they all were watching his every step. He was led to an unoccupied kennel at the end of the row that contained a bed, a blanket, a water bowl, and a dog bone.

Being young and naïve, he was easily distracted by the tasty treat. His fears subsided and he walked into the kennel, crawled onto the bed and began chomping on his very first dog bone.

3
Newfound Comforts

After a few days Rudy had adjusted easily into the routine. He learned the place he had found himself in was called an animal shelter and that the humans who ran things were kind, reliable, and even fun to be around!

On nice days he was able to spend time outside and when it got dark and cold he was always brought back in. He had toys to play with and was fed at the same time every day! These newfound comforts were things he never experienced before.

As he drifted off to sleep in this strange place, he couldn't help but wonder where Ruger was and if he was okay.

A week seemed to fly by and suddenly things changed on Rudy. He was let outside in the morning and upon returning he found his kennel empty. The girl led him to another room at the front of the building instead. She walked him to a different kennel that looked very similar to the last one. He crawled onto the bed and curled up with the new toy that was waiting for him. Although the kennel felt similar to the last one, he soon realized things were quite different.

"Okay, that's a week," announced the girl with the leash. "No one has come to claim the stray puppy, so he is officially available for adoption! I have moved him to the room for adoptable dogs and our veterinarian, Dr. Cromwell, has looked him over. He is a healthy pup and has been fully vaccinated. She will neuter him later today."

A young girl overheard the conversation between the staff members and looked up concerned.

"Neutered? What does that mean?" asked the wide-eyed girl.

"We neuter all the male dogs and cats and spay all the females before sending them to their forever homes. This is a routine procedure done by a veterinarian to ensure these animals are not able to have any more puppies or kittens. Spaying and neutering reduces both the stray dog and cat populations and the amount of animals that wind up in animal shelters."

A few days later, Rudy was led to an outdoor pen, as he had been every other day since he came to the shelter. This time, however, it was different. Another dog was already in the pen. So far in the shelter, he had not been able to meet any of the other dogs. Boy, was he excited!

He was feeling awfully lonely without having other dogs to run around with. He had seen this dog around previously and he seemed to make everyone around him smile. He had a lot of energy, and he was big! They sniffed each other's butts, like all dogs feel the need to do, and instantly became friends. The humans soon left them alone to play and that was when they started to get to know each other.

"Where did you come from?" asked the St. Bernard, Charlie.

"I'm not quite sure. I was living out there alone with my brother when one day this man came and took me here. My brother is still out there and I have no idea if he is okay. How did you end up here?"

"Hmm, a street dog. Well, I had a family...of humans, that is. They brought me home when I was just a young pup. They were so happy and I was too. They loved me and played with me and took me for walks. Things were going really well for the first few months. One day, I heard them talking about me. How I had grown so big! And that they didn't think their home was large enough and they didn't have enough time for me. They said that they didn't think it was fair to me. One day I jumped into the car like any other day thinking we were going to the lake. But, instead they brought me here."

"Wow, that's sad. So, how does this place work?" asked Rudy.

"We stay here, where we are taken care of until someone wants to adopt us," explained Charlie.

"Adopt us? What does that mean?" questioned Rudy.

"It means they take us home with them and we become part of their family. Like I was once. This family takes care of us and loves us. Some dogs are not here for very long at all while others stay longer. See Rocco, over there? He has been here the longest."

Now that Rudy was available for adoption he was able to meet all the shelter residents. He met the beagle mix named Cleo that was abandoned by her people on the side of the road. He met the intimidating, yet goofiest pit bull named Bruce. He had been transferred from an overcrowded shelter after having been saved from his first neglectful home.

Rudy even befriended some of the cats! He liked all the cats, but only a few liked him back. He was especially close with a black and white cat named Sox who was also brought in as a stray from the streets. They had a great deal in common and even knew some of the same animals on the outside!

Every time a stray animal came in Rudy tried to find out if they knew Ruger. No one had. Three full weeks had passed since Rudy was brought into the shelter and he was becoming quite comfortable with the shelter's routine. Regular meals, warm beds, and frequent play dates with other dogs were easy to get used to after fending for himself as a stray.

Although his life was a lot easier now, he still longed for a family of humans to take him home. It was very common for his shelter friends to be adopted. It was always exciting to see his friends hop into the cars of happy people and watch as they drive off to their forever homes. He wondered if his turn would ever come.

4
Love at First Sight

Winter had set in and the dogs' outdoor time dwindled to only a small part of the day. Rudy enjoyed playing in the snow but his feet would begin to get cold. Being let back inside was a nice change from his first winter when he and his brother would have to search long and hard for a warm place to sleep.

As he curled up in his bed, he began to worry about his brother. The days grew shorter, darker, and colder. How was Ruger holding up out there? Rudy drifted off to sleep dreaming of his brother.

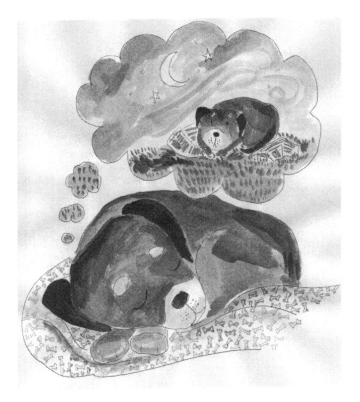

Morning came and another day at the shelter began. The day may have begun like any other, but Rudy had no idea what was in store.

Seeing that this place was an animal shelter, which housed dogs and cats looking to be adopted, people were always wandering around and meeting the different animals.

It is important to match people with the right pet. Some dogs need a lot of exercise, while others do not. There are dogs and cats that really enjoy the company of other animals, while some do best as the only pet in the home.

There are active people who are looking for a dog companion to join them on their hikes, while others are frequently away from home and an independent cat would be a better fit.

This particular day a young couple came to the shelter to see what animals were there. They knew that they wanted a large dog to join them on hikes and who also liked to cuddle. They already had a cat at home so the dog needed to be friendly with cats. Lastly, because their friends had dogs, they wanted a dog who liked other dogs as well.

They started down the hall to see all the pups. Some barked as they passed, some jumped, and some seemed to barely notice. Rudy always did the same thing when people passed his kennel. He barked! He barked loudly. His barking caused most people to keep walking. But that day, the people stopped.

They turned and read the information on his door. Several characteristics were listed under his picture.

"Active." Check.

"Good with Dogs." Check.

"Good with Cats." Check.

"Likes to Snuggle." Check.

This boy sure was meeting all of their requirements! They asked to meet him.

The staff member looped the familiar leash around Rudy's neck and led him and the couple to a little room to get acquainted.

It was love at first sight. His expressive tan eyebrows brought smiles to their faces. His long tongue hanging low made them giggle and his eagerness to climb into their laps warmed their hearts.

This was their dog! They took him for a walk and aside from needing some work on his manners he was a complete delight to be around. He was excited, he was happy, and he, too, appeared smitten.

The three of them returned to the shelter and Rudy knew what was going to happen next. He felt it. Finally, he had found his family.

They located the woman who had first introduced them and she reached for the leash. Rudy was confused. What? No, no. I'm going home with them, he thought frantically. He heard them talking, but could not understand what they were saying.

The woman took the leash and the two of them returned to his kennel. He went in and the door was shut behind him. He sat there, alone and heartbroken. It had seemed so right. They had all been so happy. What did he do to change their minds?

The sun soon set and the lights were turned off. Like so many nights before, Rudy drifted off to sleep in his kennel alone.

He woke the next day still sad and confused, but eager to see his friends. That did not happen either! Instead of heading outside for his usual morning playtime, he was kept in his kennel. What seemed like forever passed when all of a sudden the woman who had greeted him almost every morning came skipping up, smiling from ear to ear.

"Okay, buddy! Here we go!" she exclaimed. She led him outside and the couple from the day before was waiting for him! They came back! He had not messed up. He had not made them change their mind. They just needed to prepare their home for their new dog. Their new dog, Rudy!

He had witnessed this scene so many times before; happy humans leading their happy dog into the car to go to a forever home. He was now that happy dog! He hopped into the car and off they went.

He had not been in a car since the day he had arrived at the shelter. This ride was much more fun and exciting than the first one. The windows were cracked open, his ears were flapping in the wind, and smells were filling his nose.

They soon arrived at his new home. He walked in and dashed from room to room sniffing every nook and cranny. He found his water bowl and brand new dog bed. He even met the cat!

Melon, a huge long haired black cat marched out of the bedroom and pranced along the back of the couch. He watched Rudy's every move, scoping out the new family member. Rudy excitedly hopped up to greet Melon. At first Melon was a bit taken back by his eagerness, but he soon realized Rudy was not a threat.

Rudy's excitement soon turned to
exhaustion and he fell fast asleep in the giant
dog bed in the living room.

"I love everything about him! Look at
him curled up into that tiny ball! My little
Meatball," gushed his new mama.

5
Wrong All Along

The first few days were strange for Rudy. He was so happy to have a home and a family whenever they were all together. However, every time his people would leave him home alone he would panic. He had a hard time trusting that they would come back.

He had a naughty habit of chewing items that did not belong to him when left home alone. Shoes, hats, belts, and T.V. remotes all fell victim to his anxious chewing.

One particularly long stretch of time had passed with his family gone. His anxiety got the best of him and he nervously began to chew. His people returned home to find quite the scene.

A guilt-stricken dog was sitting atop a shredded bed! They were shocked but understood that his lonely, unstable past was to blame. They were determined to make him feel as comfortable and confident as they possibly could.

Within a few weeks, Rudy had made himself at home. His routine was simple and comfortable which helped him adjust and stop his nervous chewing. He was taken out for regular walks, learned some tricks, and enjoyed plenty of snuggle time with his family. He felt very loved!

As he cozied up after another fun day, he drifted off to sleep thinking about how lucky he had become. He could not help but wonder if his long lost brother, Ruger, was still out on his own fighting for his next meal and warm place to sleep.

One day, Rudy heard his people talking. They were talking about how they were always at work. They were saying they felt bad that he was stuck home alone so much. He began to worry.

He remembered hearing all this before. His friend, Charlie, the St. Bernard, had heard this from his family before he was taken to the shelter. But how could this be? Things were going so well. Then it happened. The humans called Rudy's name and motioned to the car. He reluctantly followed their orders, hopped in and they drove away.

They were smiling and acting as if they were headed somewhere fun. Rudy did not fall for it. He knew what was going on. He began to panic as they pulled into the parking lot of the animal shelter. Still smiling, his owners wandered inside while he sat anxiously in the backseat of the car.

With the windows cracked, Rudy was able to hear the chatter of several dogs. He recognized some as being his friends while he was there. That was Rocco telling jokes like usual. That was Cleo reminiscing about her old family again. But then, suddenly, Rudy heard the bark of someone he thought he would never see again.

It couldn't be... Was it?

It was Ruger! The woman with the leash casually walked Ruger out of the building and across the yard to the outdoor pen. Rudy began to squeal with excitement. Ruger must have arrived recently as he appeared uncomfortable and scared. He must not have met the other dogs yet because they would have told him this place was nothing to fear. Rudy knew he had to catch his brother's attention!

Rudy continued to make as much noise as possible from the car's backseat as the humans came outside. They instantly noticed his odd behavior. They watched him for a minute and were shocked when they heard another frantic outburst from a different dog.

They peered through the fence and their jaws dropped. Another dog, who looked strikingly similar to their own, with the same expressive tan eyebrows, was jumping up and down with his eyes locked on Rudy.

The young couple went back inside and out of Rudy's sight again. Rudy was so excited to see his brother that he had completely forgotten his fear of being dropped off at the shelter. At least he knew that his brother was okay and maybe they would be together again.

His people soon returned to the car, let Rudy out, and led him towards the shelter. Instead of heading inside, they turned and walked towards the outdoor pens...towards Ruger!

"Ruger!" cried Rudy when he reached the fence. "I can't believe it's you! Don't worry about this place. You are safe here. This is where I was taken after leaving in that car that day. All these dogs and cats live here and wait to find families of their own."

"Rudy, I'm so happy to see you! But I don't know. No one has ever been nice to us before. How can you trust them?" asked Ruger.

"There are good people out there. People who take animals into their homes and treat them as a part of their family. Please trust me. See these people here? These are my people. I have been living with them in their home and they have been taking care of me."

The woman with the leash returned and began talking with Rudy's owners.

"This boy came in as a stray. Animal Control brought him in a week ago. He was skinny and hungry and it looked as though he had been out on his own for some time. He was lucky to have been found before the weather became any colder."

"So, is he available for adoption?"

"Yes he is! No one has come looking for him, so he can now be adopted." Rudy's ears perked up at the word "adopted".

It appeared that he had been wrong all along about why they had returned to the shelter.

Rudy was not being dropped back off at the shelter after all! They had gone there to find another dog to adopt! Rudy's humans hated how often he was left alone and wanted him to have a doggy brother to keep him company. Little did they know that they would find his actual brother!

When Rudy and Ruger were reunited it was as if they had never separated. Although the humans could not understand what the pups were saying to each other, they knew in their hearts that they were meant to be together.

Before they knew it, all four of them loaded into the car and headed home. On the ride, Rudy explained to Ruger all about the wonderful people he would now call family.

They soon arrived, and Rudy and Ruger followed each other around the house and chased each other in the yard. They were thrilled to be together again. Rudy helped Ruger learn all about how to be the best pet possible and was even able to convince Ruger to befriend the cat!

Soon they were three peas in a pod.

As Rudy and Ruger curled up, just as they had when they were homeless, hungry puppies, they knew that life was finally exactly as it should be. Although much larger now, they both managed to squeeze onto the one dog bed together.

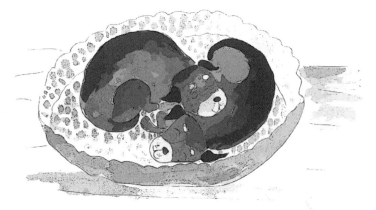

Their humans looked at each other delighted. With a huge grin, their mama exclaimed, "Look! We now have a Meatball and a Chicken Nugget!"

Hermey the Dentist (Ruger) and
King Moonracer (Rudy) on the day they
were reunited at the shelter

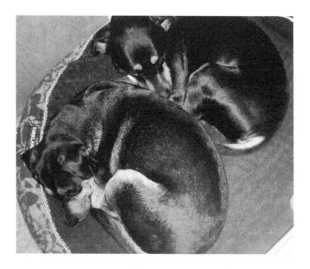

"Meatball" and "Chicken Nugget"
sharing a bed

Hermey, Mellow (Melon), and King:
Three peas in a pod

About the Author

Lisa Spaulding began working at her local animal shelter in March 2015 as a shelter technician focusing on animal care, behavioral observations, potential adopter-animal introductions, and hosting kids for tours and programs. Upon adopting her second dog shortly after joining the staff, she was inspired to write a children's book that filled in the holes of her once stray dogs' pasts. She resides in Colorado with her husband Jeffrey where she loves to take in the natural beauty that surrounds her.

About the Illustrator

Bonnie Wiegand lives in Colorado with her husband John and doggy Jack. When Jack was a puppy, he lived at the Second Chance Human Society in Ridgeway, CO. Now he's part of the family! When Bonnie is not drawing or painting, you might find her out in the woods on a hike.

****

Lisa enjoyed bringing this first book to life so much that she decided to continue down the road of story telling to create a collection of shelter stories. Like the first book, true events and actual animals she has cared for at the shelter will inspire each new story. Bonnie, of course, will do all the illustrating!
Be sure to check out all other shelter adventures in
The From Alone to A Home Collection!